KU-186-954

SPACE CORPS

TONY LEE AND RYAN PENTNEY

EDGE
FRANKLIN WATTS
LONDON·SYDNEY

"HIT HIM WITH YOUR LIGHT SWORD!"
"I WILL ONCE YOU STOP SHOOTING ME!"
EDDIE, STOP HITTING ALL THE BUTTONS! YOU'RE NOT HELPING!
I AM HELPING! I'M THE BEST HELPER EVER!
AND EVERYONE KNOWS THAT HITTING BUTTONS --
I DON'T BELIEVE IT!
-- WE COMPLETED THE GAME!

I FINISHED THE GAME! I AM THE BEST!
THAT'S NOT FAIR! I'VE BEEN PLAYING THIS GAME FOR HOURS!
YOU ONLY TURNED UP TWENTY MINUTES AGO!
PLAYING GAMES IS BORING. WINNING GAMES IS BEST!
I WON THAT GAME! YOU ONLY HELPED!
YOU ONLY WON BECAUSE I PLAYED!
PLAYED? ALL YOU DID WAS MASH BUTTONS TOGETHER!
MUM! ALEX IS PICKING ON ME!
ALL I WANTED WAS A DOG. NOT A BROTHER.

ALEX - YOUR BROTHER SAYS THAT YOU'RE TAKING CREDIT FOR **HIS** GAME SCORE.
THAT'S NOT TRUE!
I PLAYED IT FROM THE START - EDDIE ONLY JOINED IN DURING THE LAST BATTLE!
IT'S ONLY A GAME. IT DOESN'T MATTER WHO WON.
YEAH. EVEN IF IT **WAS** ME.
NOT HELPING.
YOU CAN'T HELP IT IF YOU'RE **RUBBISH** AT GAMES.
MUM, EDDIE FELL DOWN THE STAIRS.
WHEN?
IN ABOUT FIVE MINUTES FROM NOW!
I'M GOING TO MY ROOM!
IT'S MY ROOM, TOO!

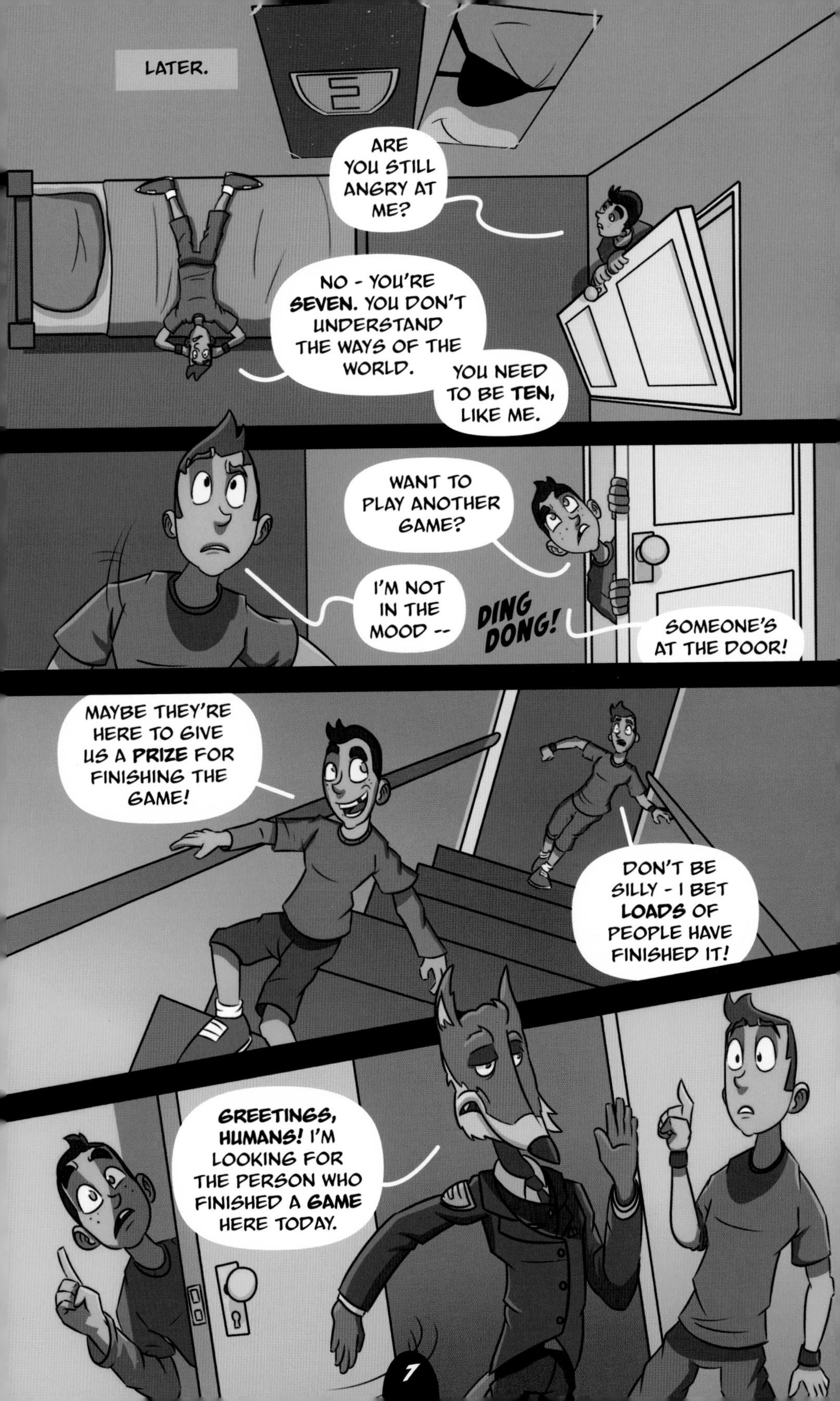
LATER.
ARE YOU STILL ANGRY AT ME?
NO - YOU'RE SEVEN. YOU DON'T UNDERSTAND THE WAYS OF THE WORLD.
YOU NEED TO BE TEN, LIKE ME.
WANT TO PLAY ANOTHER GAME?
I'M NOT IN THE MOOD --
DING DONG!
SOMEONE'S AT THE DOOR!
MAYBE THEY'RE HERE TO GIVE US A PRIZE FOR FINISHING THE GAME!
DON'T BE SILLY - I BET LOADS OF PEOPLE HAVE FINISHED IT!
GREETINGS, HUMANS! I'M LOOKING FOR THE PERSON WHO FINISHED A GAME HERE TODAY.

I'M AGENT FOX OF THE SPACE CORPS. I'M LOOKING FOR ALEXEDDIE.
ALEX EDDIE?
YOU ADDED YOUR NAME TO MY GAMER PROFILE.
MUM SAID I WAS TOO YOUNG FOR MY OWN!
I'M ALEX. THIS IS EDDIE. WE WERE BOTH PLAYING THE GAME.
THAT'S IMPOSSIBLE! THE GAME DOESN'T HAVE A TWO-PLAYER SETTING!
YEAH, I DIDN'T THINK HE WAS PLAYING EITHER, HE WAS JUST HITTING BUTTONS -
- BUT HE DEFINITELY WAS PLAYING AT THE END.
IS YOUR TAIL REAL?

NOBODY HAS EVER COMPLETED THE GAME BEFORE.
IT'S ACTUALLY A TEST, TO GET INTO THE **SPACE CORPS** - AND YOU TWO HAVE PASSED!
REALLY?
WOAH!
MUM, CAN EDDIE AND I GO TO THE SPACE CORPS BASE WITH A **TALKING FOX?**
OF COURSE, DEAR. BUT FINISH PLAYING BY DINNER.
SHE SAID YES!
EXCELLENT! SO GATHER CLOSE AND I'LL ENGAGE THE TELEPORTER--
-- TO TAKE US TO THE **SPACE CORPS!**

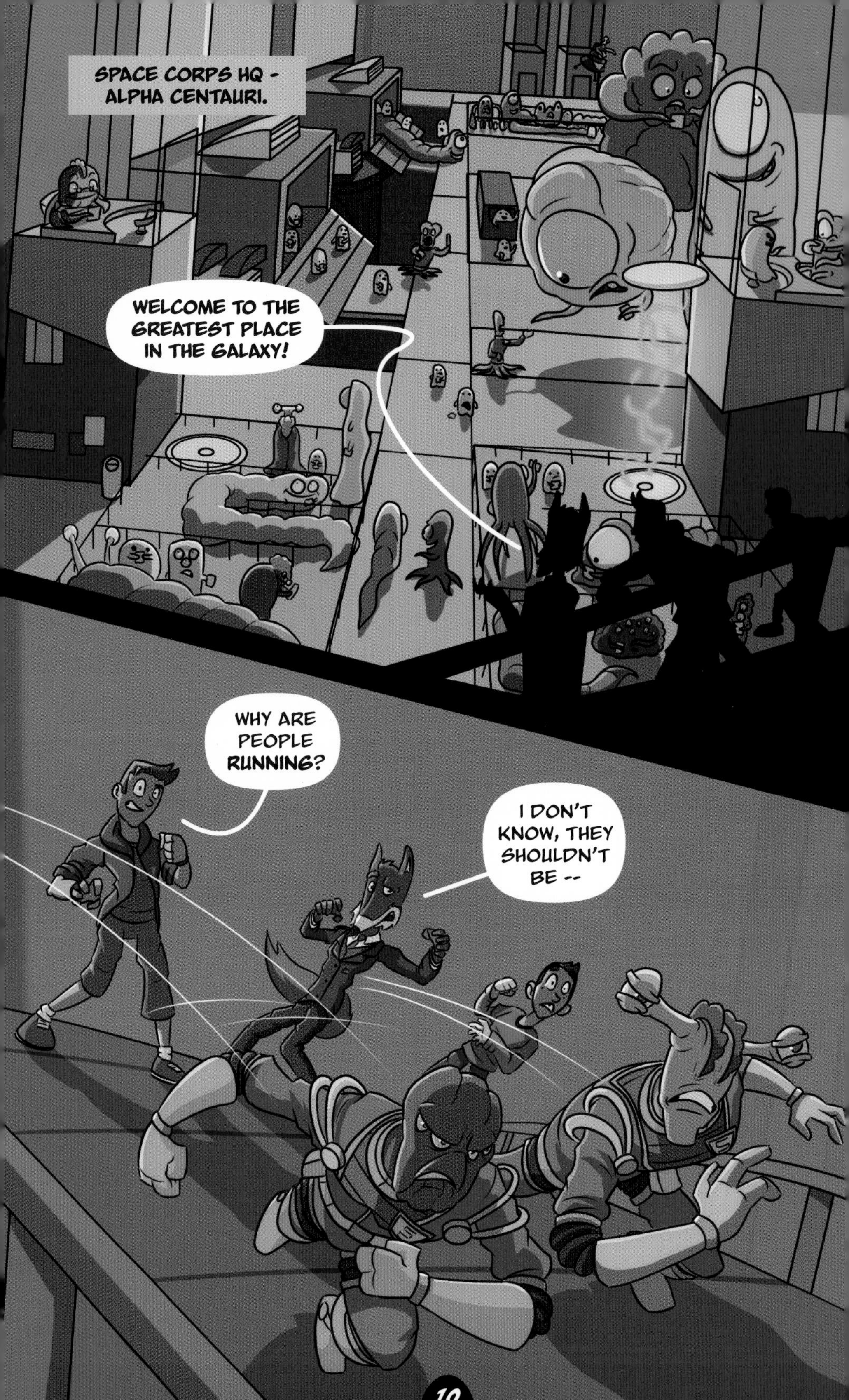
SPACE CORPS HQ - ALPHA CENTAURI.
WELCOME TO THE GREATEST PLACE IN THE GALAXY!
WHY ARE PEOPLE RUNNING?
I DON'T KNOW, THEY SHOULDN'T BE --

THE BADNESS ARE ATTACKING. THEY HAVE A NEW ICE WEAPON.
WE'RE GOING TO STOP IT BEFORE THEY CAN USE IT.
WHO ARE THE TINY HUMANS?
ALEX AND EDDIE - THEY FINISHED THE GAME.
THEN THEY MUST BE SPECIAL INDEED!
I AM SPACE CAT. THAT IS DIMENSION DOG.
WITH OUR FRIENDS TIME SQUIRREL AND GRAVITY BEAR, WE SAVE THE COSMOS.
I LIKE YOUR NECKLACE!
IT'S NOT REALLY A NECKLACE. WE BOTH HAVE ONE - TWO OF THE LAST ETERNITY STONES IN EXISTENCE.

RUMBLE!
QUICK! TO MY SPACESHIP!
WHY NOT MY SHIP?
BECAUSE YOURS SMELLS OF DOG.
AND YOURS SMELLS OF KITTY LITTER!
STOP THIS! YOU'RE BEST FRIENDS!
CATS ARE NOT FRIENDS WITH DOGS. THEY ARE DUMB!
WE'RE NOT! IT'S JUST AN ACT SO THAT YOU DON'T FEEL EVEN MORE DUMB!
CAN WE JUST PICK A SHIP!
WHACK

ON THE BADNESS BATTLECRUISER...
YOUR EVILNESS! THE WEAPON IS READY TO FIRE!
THEN GET ON WITH IT --
GRAVITY BEAR, IS YOUR SHIP REPAIRED? IT'S THE BIGGEST ONE WE HAVE.
IT IS! COME ON --
-- FIRE!
FOOOOM!

FZZZSHHH!
GRAVITY BEAR!
THE BADNESS HAVE PERFECTED THE ICE BEAM!
IT'LL FREEZE EVERYTHING IN ITS PATH!
WE NEED TO SPLIT UP. I'LL GATHER INFORMATION FROM THE AIR. I'LL TAKE THE SMALLEST HUMAN -
- YOU GET TO THE NEXUS CANNON!
AGREED! I'LL TAKE THE BIGGER HUMAN.
THIS ISN'T AS FUN AS THE GAME.
I HOPE GRAVITY BEAR IS OKAY.

WHO ARE THE BADNESS?
THE WORST ALIEN RACES IN THE GALAXY, ALL JOINED TOGETHER.
THE SPACE CORPS AND THE FABLED FIVE* ARE THE ONLY TEAMS THAT FIGHT THEM.
PEW!
PEW!
PEW!
QUICK! WE'RE UNDER ATTACK! TO THE GUNS!
PEW!
BUT I'VE NEVER DONE THIS BEFORE! ALEX WAS RIGHT - I JUST HIT THE BUTTONS!
*SEE 'MISTER CLIP-CLOP - INTERGALACTIC SPACE UNICORN'

PEW!
PEW!
THEY'RE DRONES! NOBODY IS ACTUALLY IN THEM!
OH.
WELL, THAT'S ALL RIGHT THEN.
PEW!
PEW!
GOOD WORK, EDDIE THE DESTROYER! NOW I JUST NEED TO GET SOME READINGS ON THEIR ICE WEAPON --
FOOM!

FOOM!
LOOK OUT! THE BATTLESHIP IS FIRING THE ICE BEAM AT US!
FOOOSH!
YES! THE ICE BEAM BLEW UP THE LAST DRONE - BUT IT ALSO HIT OUR RIGHT-SIDE ENGINES!
WE'RE GOING DOWN!
BUCKLE UP, KID!

SPACE CORPS HQ.
THERE ARE TOO MANY! WE NEED TO DISTRACT THEM SO WE CAN REACH THE NEXUS!
HOW?
LASER POINTERS. CATNIP. MICE.
NO, THAT WON'T WORK ON THEM --
THE ICE BEAM FREEZES THINGS, RIGHT? WHAT IF IT FROZE WATER?
CATS HATE WATER - BUT I LIKE YOUR IDEA, CADET BIGGER HUMAN!
MY NAME IS ALEX.
AIM FOR THE WATER TOWER!

PEW!
PEW!
PEW!
PEW!
BRING THAT WATER TOWER DOWN!
RUNCH!
SPLOOSH!
WE JUST NEED TO GET THE ICE BEAM TO HIT THE WATER!
WHOEVER DRAWS THEIR FIRE WILL BE FROZEN TOO!

HOLD THE TINY HUMAN WHILE I --
NO - YOU NEED TO GET TO THE NEXUS!
FOR SPACE CORPS!
JUST REMEMBER TO THAW US OUT!
HEY! BADNESS! YOU SMELL SO BAD --
FOOOSH!

CRACKLE!
THE ICE HAS TRAPPED ME! GET ME A CUTTER SO I CAN --
WHAP!
THEIR ARMY IS FROZEN - THANKS TO THIS TINY HUMAN - AND TIME SQUIRREL'S BRAVERY!
NOW WE FIGHT OUR WAY TO THE NEXUS!

ELSEWHERE ON THE BASE.
SO WHAT IS THE NEXUS?
IT'S AN ENERGY CANNON WHERE THE THIRD, RED ETERNITY STONE IS HOUSED.
IT CAN STOP MOST THINGS.
MOST THINGS?
IT WON'T WORK AGAINST THE BADNESS BATTLESHIP - I TOOK SOME READINGS BEFORE WE WERE HIT.
PEW!
ONLY A FORCE OF WHITE LIGHT ENERGY CAN DO THAT.
THE NEXUS ONLY FIRES RED LIGHT ENERGY.
WHY IS EVERYTHING COVERED IN ICE?

THE NEXUS.
THE ETERNITY STONE WILL TAKE OUT THE BATTLESHIP! FIRE!
KRAK-OOOM!
HA! THEIR WEAPON IS USELESS!
PREPARE TO DESTROY EVERYTHING! COVER THE WHOLE WORLD IN ICE!

I DON'T UNDERSTAND...
IT NEEDS TO BE WHITE ENERGY.
EDDIE! YOU'RE ALIVE!
NOW YOU TELL US! ALWAYS COMING IN AT THE LAST MINUTE!
I ALMOST GOT KILLED GAINING THEIR POWER READINGS!
WITHOUT ME WE WOULDN'T KNOW IT NEEDS TO BE WHITE LIGHT!
WHICH WE DON'T HAVE! SO WE'RE DOOMED!
WELL IF WE'RE DOOMED, I DON'T WANT TO SPEND MY LAST MOMENTS WITH AN IDIOT CAT --
WILL YOU BOTH STOP THIS! PLEASE!

ALL MY LIFE I'VE LOVED THE SPACE CORPS GAMES - BECAUSE YOU'RE A FAMILY!
EVERYONE WORKS TOGETHER - AND HERE EVERYONE'S A FRIEND!
JUST LIKE ME AND EDDIE. HE MIGHT ANNOY ME - BUT HE'S MY BROTHER.
AND TOGETHER WE'LL BEAT ANYTHING. JUST LIKE THE GAME.
TOGETHER WE'RE THE BEST.
HE'S RIGHT. WE NEED TO WORK TOGETHER.
WHAT ABOUT OUR ETERNITY STONES?
ALONE, THEY'RE JUST NECKLACES. POWERLESS.
BUT TOGETHER - MAYBE THEY CAN DO SOMETHING MORE!

OF COURSE! SHONE THROUGH BLUE, RED AND GREEN FILTERS --
WE GET BLINDING WHITE LIGHT!
YOU KNOW IF THIS FAILS, WE'LL PROBABLY ALL DIE.
YEAH - BUT THERE ARE WORSE ANIMALS TO DIE BESIDE.
YEAH. LIKE BADGERS!
HAHAHA!
HMMMMMMMMMMM

FWAASSSHHH
KRAK-OOM!
OUR SHIELDS ARE GONE! ABANDON SHIP!

BADA-BOOM!

COME ON, BADNESS - YOU'RE GOING TO SPACE JAIL!

TIME SQUIRREL! GRAVITY BEAR! YOU'RE ALIVE!
ALL THANKS TO YOU, ALEX AND EDDIE.
WORTHY ADDITIONS TO THE SPACE CORPS!
YEAH, ABOUT THAT.
I THINK I'D LIKE TO GO HOME.
ME TOO. I MISS MY MUM.
I UNDERSTAND. BUT, IF YOU EVER CHANGE YOUR MINDS, THERE'S ALWAYS A PLACE HERE FOR YOU.
BUT IF YOU ARE LEAVING --
-- THEN WE HAVE A VERY IMPORTANT FAVOUR TO ASK YOU.
INDEED.

BACK ON EARTH.
USE THE ELECTRO-LEAD!
GOOD IDEA! AND YOU CAN CALL TIME SQUIRREL!
EDDIE - YOU WERE RIGHT. IT IS BETTER TO PLAY GAMES WITH SOMEONE THAN ALONE.
ALTHOUGH I'M STILL BETTER THAN YOU!
YOU COME IN AT THE END! IT'S ALWAYS EASIER AT THE END!
THEN WHY CAN'T YOU EVER FINISH THE GAME?
BOYS! DINNER!
NEXT TIME, CADET EDDIE.
SEE YOU THERE, CADET ALEX!

I'VE BEEN MEANING TO ASK, BOYS - WHERE DID YOU GET THE PENDANTS?
WE WERE GIVEN THEM, DAD - THEY'RE ETERNITY STONES!
IT'S SO THEY'RE SAFE IF THE SPACE CORPS GET ATTACKED AGAIN!
I THINK THEY CAME WITH THE EXPANSION PACK.
OH.
AND IT MEANS WE CAN MAKE SURE YOU'RE SAFE, TINY HUMANS.
SO, WHERE NOW?
RAVEN SABLEMANE IS HAVING A BIRTHDAY PARTY. WE COULD GO?

YOU MEAN THE SPACE UNICORN? SURE, WHY NOT.
THEY THINK THEY'RE SO CLEVER. BUT THEY HAVEN'T DEFEATED THE BADNESS YET!
SOON WE SHALL GAIN EVEN MORE ALIENS TO OUR SIDE - AND WE SHALL BE INVINCIBLE!
HAHAHAHA
THE END?